D0805009

THE ADVENTURES OF OLD MR. TOAD

THE ADVENTURES OF OLD MR. TOAD

THORNTON W. BURGESS

Cover Illustration by
Tricia Zimic

AERIE

Contents

Contents

I

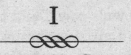

Jimmy Skunk Is Puzzled

Old Mother West Wind had just come down from the Purple Hills and turned loose her children, the Merry Little Breezes, from the big bag in which she had been carrying them. They were very lively and very merry as they danced and raced across the Green Meadows in all directions, for it was good to be back there once more. Old Mother West Wind almost sighed as she watched them for a few minutes. She felt that she would like to join them. Always the springtime made her feel this way,—young, mad, carefree, and happy. But she had work to do. She had to turn the windmill to pump water for

Farmer Brown's cows, and this was only one of many mills standing idle as they waited for her. So she puffed her cheeks out and started about her business.

Jimmy Skunk sat at the top of the hill that overlooks the Green Meadows and watched her out of sight. Then he started to amble down the Lone Little Path to look for some beetles. He was ambling along in his lazy way, for you know he never hurries, when he heard someone puffing and blowing behind him. Of course he turned to see who it was, and he was greatly surprised when he discovered Old Mr. Toad. Yes, Sir, it was Old Mr. Toad, and he seemed in a great hurry. He was quite short of breath, but he was hopping along in the most determined way as if he were in a great hurry to get somewhere.

Now it is a very unusual thing for Mr. Toad to hurry, very unusual indeed. As a rule he hops a few steps and then sits down to think it over. Jimmy had never before seen him hop more than a few steps unless he was trying to get away from danger, from Mr. Blacksnake for instance. Of course the first thing Jimmy thought of was Mr. Blacksnake, and he looked for him. But there was no sign of Mr. Blacksnake or of any other danger. Then he looked very hard at Old Mr. Toad, and he saw right away that Old Mr. Toad didn't seem to be frightened at all, only very determined, and as if he had something important on his mind.

"Well, well," exclaimed Jimmy Skunk, "whatever has got into those long hind legs of yours to make them work so fast?"

Old Mr. Toad didn't say a word, but simply tried to get past Jimmy and keep on his way. Jimmy put out one hand and turned Old Mr. Toad right over on his back, where he kicked and struggled in an effort to get on his feet again, and looked very ridiculous.

"Don't you know that it isn't polite not to speak when you are spoken to?" demanded Jimmy severely, though his eyes twinkled.

"I—I beg your pardon. I didn't have any breath to spare," panted Old Mr. Toad. "You see I'm in a great hurry."

"Yes, I see," replied Jimmy. "But don't you know that it isn't good for the health to hurry so? Now, pray, what are you in such a hurry for? I don't see anything to run away from."

"I'm not running away," retorted Old Mr. Toad indignantly. "I've business to attend to at the Smiling Pool, and I'm late as it is."

"Business!" exclaimed Jimmy as if he could hardly believe his ears. "What business have you at the Smiling Pool?"

4

"That is my own affair," retorted Old Mr. Toad, "but if you really want to know, I'll tell you. I have a very important part in the spring chorus, and I'm going down there to sing. I have a very beautiful voice."

That was too much for Jimmy Skunk. He just lay down and rolled over and over with laughter. The idea of any one so homely, almost ugly-looking as Mr. Toad thinking that he had a beautiful voice! "Ha, ha, ha! Ho, ho, ho!" roared Jimmy.

When at last he stopped because he couldn't laugh anymore, he discovered that Old Mr. Toad was on his way again. Hop, hop, hipperty-hop, hop, hop, hipperty-hop went Mr. Toad. Jimmy watched him, and he confessed that he was puzzled.

II

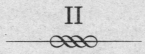

Jimmy Skunk Consults His Friends

Jimmy Skunk scratched his head
thoughtfully as he watched Old Mr.
Toad go down the Lone Little Path,
hop, hop, hipperty-hop, towards the Smiling Pool. He certainly was puzzled, was
Jimmy Skunk. If Old Mr. Toad had told
him that he could fly, Jimmy would not
have been more surprised, or found it
harder to believe than that Old Mr. Toad
had a beautiful voice. The truth is,
Jimmy didn't believe it. He thought that
Old Mr. Toad was trying to fool him.

Presently Peter Rabbit came along. He
found Jimmy Skunk sitting in a brown
study. He had quite forgotten to look for
fat beetles, and when he forgets to do

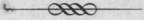

that you may make up your mind that
Jimmy is doing some hard thinking.

"Hello, old Striped-coat, what have
you got on your mind this fine morning?"
cried Peter Rabbit.

"Him," said Jimmy simply, pointing
down the Lone Little Path.

Peter looked. "Do you mean Old Mr.
Toad?" he asked.

Jimmy nodded. "Do you see anything
queer about him?" he asked in his turn.

Peter stared down the Lone Little
Path. "No," he replied, "except that he
seems in a great hurry."

"That's just it," Jimmy returned
promptly. "Did you ever see him hurry unless he was frightened?"

Peter confessed that he never had.

"Well, he isn't frightened now, yet just
look at him go," retorted Jimmy. "Says
he has got a beautiful voice, and that he

7

has to take part in the spring chorus at the Smiling Pool and that he is late."

Peter looked very hard at Jimmy to see if he was fooling or telling the truth. Then he began to laugh. "Old Mr. Toad sing! The very idea!" he cried. "He can sing about as much as I can, and that is not at all."

Jimmy grinned. "I think he's crazy, if you ask me," said he. "And yet he was just as earnest about it as if it were really so. I think he must have eaten something that has gone to his head. There's Unc' Billy Possum over there. Let's ask him what he thinks."

So Jimmy and Peter joined Unc' Billy, and Jimmy told the story about Old Mr. Toad all over again. Unc' Billy chuckled and laughed just as they had at the idea of Old Mr. Toad's saying he had a beautiful voice. But Unc' Billy has a shrewd little head on his shoulders. After a few minutes he stopped laughing.

"Ah done learn a right smart long time ago that Ah don' know all there is to know about mah neighbors," said he. "We-uns done think of Brer Toad as ugly-lookin' fo' so long that we-uns may have overlooked something. Ah don' reckon Brer Toad can sing, but Ah 'lows that perhaps he thinks he can. What do you-alls say to we-uns going down to the Smiling Pool and finding out what he really is up to?"

"The very thing!" cried Peter, kicking up his heels. You know Peter is always ready to go anywhere or do anything that will satisfy his curiosity.

Jimmy Skunk thought it over for a few minutes, and then he decided that as he hadn't anything in particular to do, and as he might find some fat beetles on the

9

way, he would go too. So off they started after Old Mr. Toad, Peter Rabbit in the lead as usual, Unc' Billy Possum next, grinning as only he can grin, and in the rear Jimmy Skunk, taking his time and keeping a sharp eye out for fat beetles.

III

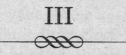

The Hunt for Old Mr. Toad

Now, though Old Mr. Toad was hurrying as fast as ever he could and was quite out of breath, he wasn't getting along very fast compared with the way Peter Rabbit or Jimmy Skunk or Unc' Billy Possum could cover the ground. You see he cannot make long jumps like his cousin, Grandfather Frog, but only little short hops.

So Peter and Jimmy and Unc' Billy took their time about following him. They stopped to hunt for fat beetles for Jimmy Skunk, and at every little patch of sweet clover for Peter Rabbit to help himself. Once they wasted a lot of time while Unc' Billy Possum hunted for a

nest of Carol the Meadowlark, on the chance that he would find some fresh eggs there. He didn't find the nest for the very good reason that Carol hadn't built one yet. Peter was secretly glad. You know he doesn't eat eggs, and he is always sorry for his feathered friends when their eggs are stolen.

Half way across the Green Meadows they stopped to play with the Merry Little Breezes, and because it was very pleasant there, they played longer than they realized. When at last they started on again, Old Mr. Toad was out of sight. You see all the time he had kept right on going, hop, hop, hipperty-hop.

"Never mind," said Peter, "we can catch up with him easy enough, he's such a slow-poke."

But even a slow-poke who keeps right on doing a thing without wasting any time always gets somewhere sooner or later, very often sooner than those who are naturally quicker, but who waste their time. So it was with Old Mr. Toad. He kept right on, hop, hop, hipperty-hop, while the others were playing, and so it happened that when at last Peter and Jimmy and Unc' Billy reached the Smiling Pool, they hadn't caught another glimpse of Old Mr. Toad.

"Do you suppose he hid somewhere, and we passed him?" asked Peter.

Unc' Billy shook his head. "Ah don' reckon so," said he. "We-uns done been foolin' away our time, an' Brer Toad done stole a march on us. Ah reckons we-uns will find him sittin' on the bank here somewhere."

So right away the three separated to look for Old Mr. Toad. All along the bank of the Smiling Pool they looked. They peeped under old leaves and sticks. They looked in every place where Old Mr.

Toad might have hidden, but not a trace of him did they find.

"Tra-la-la-lee! Oka-chee! Oka-chee!
Happy am I as I can be!"

sang Mr. Redwing, as he swayed to and fro among the bulrushes.

"Say, Mr. Redwing, have you seen Old Mr. Toad?" called Peter Rabbit.

"No," replied Mr. Redwing. "Is that whom you fellows are looking for? I wondered if you had lost something. What do you want with Old Mr. Toad?"

Peter explained how they had followed Old Mr. Toad just to see what he really was up to. "Of course we know that he hasn't any more voice than I have," declared Peter, "but we are curious to know if he really thinks he has, and why he should be in such a hurry to reach the

Smiling Pool. It looks to us as if the spring has made Old Mr. Toad crazy."

"Oh, that's it, is it?" replied Mr. Redwing, his bright eyes twinkling. "Some people don't know as much as they might. I've been wondering where Old Mr. Toad was, and I'm ever so glad to learn that he hasn't forgotten that he has a very important part in our beautiful spring chorus." Then once more Mr. Redwing began to sing.

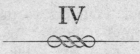

IV

PETER RABBIT FINDS OLD MR. TOAD

It isn't often that Peter Rabbit is truly envious, but sometimes in the joyousness of spring he is. He envies the birds because they can pour out in beautiful song the joy that is in them. The only way he can express his feelings is by kicking his long heels, jumping about, and such foolish things. While that gives Peter a great deal of satisfaction, it doesn't add to the joy of other people as do the songs of the birds, and you know to give joy to others is to add to your own joy. So there are times when Peter wishes he could sing.

He was wishing this very thing now, as he sat on the bank of the Smiling Pool, listening to the great spring chorus.

"Tra-la-la-lee! Oka-chee! Oka-chee!
 There's joy in the spring for you and for me."

sang Redwing the Blackbird from the bulrushes.

From over in the Green Meadows rose the clear lilt of Carol the Meadowlark, and among the alders just where the Laughing Brook ran into the Smiling Pool a flood of happiness was pouring from the throat of Little Friend the Song Sparrow. Winsome Bluebird's sweet, almost plaintive, whistle seemed to fairly float in the air, so that it was hard to say just where it did come from, and in the top of the Big Hickory-tree, Welcome Robin was singing as if his heart were bursting with joy. Even Sammy Jay was adding a beautiful, bell-like note instead

17

of his usual harsh scream. As for the Smiling Pool, it seemed as if the very water itself sang, for a mighty chorus of clear piping voices from unseen singers rose from all around its banks. Peter knew who those singers were, although look as he would he could see none of them. They were hylas, the tiny cousins of Sticky-toes the Tree Toad.

Listening to all these joyous voices, Peter forgot for a time what had brought him to the Smiling Pool. But Jimmy Skunk and Unc' Billy Possum didn't forget. They were still hunting for Old Mr. Toad.

"Well, old Mr. Dreamer, have you found him yet?" asked Jimmy Skunk, stealing up behind Peter and poking him in the back.

Peter came to himself with a start. "No," said he. "I was just listening and wishing that I could sing, too. Don't you ever wish you could sing, Jimmy?"

"No," replied Jimmy, "I never waste time wishing I could do things it was never meant I should do. It's funny where Old Mr. Toad is. He said that he was coming down here to sing, and Redwing the Blackbird seemed to be expecting him. I've looked everywhere I can think of without finding him, but I don't believe in giving up without another try. Stop your dreaming and come help us hunt."

So Peter stopped his dreaming and joined in the search. Now there was one place where neither Peter nor Jimmy nor Unc' Billy had thought of looking. That was in the Smiling Pool itself. They just took it for granted that Old Mr. Toad was somewhere on the bank. Presently Peter came to a place where the bank was very low and the water was shallow

for quite a little distance out in the Smiling Pool. From out of that shallow water came the piping voice of a hyla, and Peter stopped to stare, trying to see the tiny singer.

Suddenly he jumped right up in the air with surprise. There was a familiar-looking head sticking out of the water. Peter had found Old Mr. Toad!

V

OLD MR. TOAD'S MUSIC BAG

Never think that you have learned
  All there is to know.
That's the surest way of all
  Ignorance to show.

I've found Old Mr. Toad!" cried Peter Rabbit, hurrying after Jimmy Skunk.

"Where?" demanded Jimmy.

"In the water," declared Peter. "He's sitting right over there where the water is shallow, and he didn't notice me at all. Let's get Unc' Billy, and then creep over to the edge of the Smiling Pool and watch to see if Old Mr. Toad really does try to sing."

So they hunted up Unc' Billy Possum, and the three stole very softly over to the edge of the Smiling Pool, where the bank was low and the water shallow. Sure enough, there sat Old Mr. Toad with just his head out of water. And while they were watching him, something very strange happened.

"What—what's the matter with him?" whispered Peter, his big eyes looking as if they might pop out of his head.

"If he don't watch out, he'll blow up and bust!" exclaimed Jimmy.

"Listen!" whispered Unc' Billy Possum. "Do mah ol' ears hear right? 'Pears to me that that song is coming right from where Brer Toad is sitting."

It certainly did appear so, and of all the songs that glad spring day there was none sweeter. Indeed there were few as sweet. The only trouble was the song was so very short. It lasted only for two

or three seconds. And when it ended,
Old Mr. Toad looked quite his natural
self again; just as commonplace, almost
ugly, as ever. Peter looked at Jimmy
Skunk, Jimmy looked at Unc' Billy Possum, and Unc' Billy looked at Peter. And
no one had a word to say. Then all three
looked back at Old Mr. Toad.

And even as they looked, his throat
began to swell and swell and swell, until
it was no wonder that Jimmy Skunk had
thought that he was in danger of blowing up. And then, when it stopped swelling, there came again those beautiful
little notes, so sweet and tremulous that
Peter actually held his breath to listen.
There was no doubt that Old Mr. Toad
was singing just as he had said he was
going to, and it was just as true that his
song was one of the sweetest if not *the*
sweetest of all the chorus from and
around the Smiling Pool. It was very

hard to believe, but Peter and Jimmy and Unc' Billy both saw and heard, and that was enough. Their respect for Old Mr. Toad grew tremendously as they listened.

"How does he do it?" whispered Peter.

"With that bag under his chin, of course," replied Jimmy Skunk. "Don't you see it's only when that is swelled out that he sings? It's a regular music bag. And I didn't know he had any such bag there at all."

"I wish," said Peter Rabbit, feeling of his throat, "that I had a music bag like that in my throat."

And then he joined in the laugh of Jimmy and Unc' Billy, but still with something of a look of wistfulness in his eyes.

VI

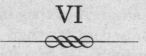

PETER DISCOVERS SOMETHING MORE

There are stranger things in the world to-day
  Than ever you dreamed could be.
There's beauty in some of the commonest
    things
  If only you've eyes to see.

Ever since Peter Rabbit was a little chap and had first run away from home, he had known Old Mr. Toad, and never once had Peter suspected that he could sing. Also he had thought Old Mr. Toad almost ugly-looking, and he knew that most of his neighbors thought the same way. They were fond of Old Mr. Toad, for he was always good-natured and attended strictly

to his own affairs; but they liked to poke fun at him, and as for there being anything beautiful about him, such a thing never entered their heads.

Now that they had discovered that he really has a very beautiful voice, they began to look on him with a great deal more respect. This was especially so with Peter. He got in the habit of going over to the Smiling Pool every day, when the way was clear, just to sit on the bank and listen to Old Mr. Toad.

"Why didn't you ever tell us before that you could sing?" he asked one day, as Old Mr. Toad looked up at him from the Smiling Pool.

"What was the use of wasting my breath?" demanded Old Mr. Toad. "You wouldn't have believed me if I had. You didn't believe me when I did tell you."

Peter knew that this was true, and he couldn't find any answer ready. At last he

ventured another question. "Why haven't
I ever heard you sing before?"

"You have," replied Old Mr. Toad
tartly. "I sang right in this very place
last spring, and the spring before, and
the spring before that. You've sat on that
very bank lots of times while I was singing. The trouble with you, Peter, is that
you don't use your eyes or your ears."

Peter looked more foolish than ever.
But he ventured another question. It
wouldn't be Peter to let a chance for
questions go by. "Have I ever heard you
singing up on the meadows or in the Old
Orchard?"

"No," replied Old Mr. Toad, "I only
sing in the springtime. That's the time
for singing. I just *have* to sing then. In
the summer it is too hot, and in the winter I sleep. I always return to my old
home to sing. You know I was born here.

27

All my family gathers in the spring to sing, so of course I come too."

Old Mr. Toad filled out his queer music bag under his chin and began to sing again. Peter watched him. Now it just happened that Old Mr. Toad was facing him, and so Peter looked down straight into his eyes. He never had looked into Mr. Toad's eyes before, and now he just stared and stared, for it came over him that those eyes were very beautiful, very beautiful indeed.

"Oh!" he exclaimed, "what beautiful eyes you have, Mr. Toad!"

"So I've been told before," replied Old Mr. Toad. "My family always has had beautiful eyes. There is an old saying that every Toad has jewels in his head, but of course he hasn't, not real jewels. It is just the beautiful eyes. Excuse me, Peter, but I'm needed in that chorus." Old

Mr. Toad once more swelled out his throat and began to sing.

Peter watched him a while longer, then hopped away to the dear Old Briarpatch, and he was very thoughtful.

"Never again I will I call anybody homely and ugly until I know all about him," said Peter, which was a very wise decision. Don't you think so?

VII

A Shadow Passes Over the
Smiling Pool

Here's what Mr. Toad says;
Heed it well, my dear:
"Time to watch for clouds is
When the sky is clear."

He says that that is the reason
that he lives to a good old age,
does Old Mr. Toad. I suppose he
means that when the sky is cloudy,
everybody is looking for rain and is prepared for it, but when the sun is shining,
most people forget that there is such a
thing as a storm, so when it comes suddenly very few are prepared for it. It is
the same way with danger and trouble.
So Old Mr. Toad very wisely watches out

when there seems to be the least need of it, and he finds it always pays.

It was a beautiful spring evening. Over back of the Purple Hills to which Old Mother West Wind had taken her children, the Merry Little Breezes, and behind which jolly, round, red Mr. Sun had gone to bed, there was still a faint, clear light. But over the Green Meadows and the Smiling Pool the shadows had drawn a curtain of soft dusk which in the Green Forest became black. The little stars looked down from the sky and twinkled just to see their reflections twinkle back at them from the Smiling Pool. And there and all around it was perfect peace. Jerry Muskrat swam back and forth, making little silver lines on the surface of the Smiling Pool and squeaking contentedly, for it was the hour which he loves best. Little Friend the Song Sparrow had tucked his head

31

under his wing and gone to sleep among the alders along the Laughing Brook and Redwing the Blackbird had done the same thing among the bulrushes. All the feathered songsters who had made joyous the bright day had gone to bed.

But this did not mean that the glad spring chorus was silent. Oh, my, no! No indeed! The Green Meadows were silent, and the Green Forest was silent, but as if to make up for this, the sweet singers of the Smiling Pool, the hylas and the frogs and Old Mr. Toad, were pouring out their gladness as if they had not been singing most of the departed day. You see it was the hour they love best of all, the hour which seems to them just made for singing, and they were doing their best to tell Old Mother Nature how they love her, and how glad they were that she had brought back sweet Mistress Spring to waken them from their long sleep.

It was so peaceful and beautiful there that it didn't seem possible that danger of any kind could be lurking near. But Old Mr. Toad, swelling out that queer music bag in his throat and singing with all his might, never once forgot that wise saying of his, and so he was the first to see what looked like nothing so much as a little detached bit of the blackness of the Green Forest floating out towards the Smiling Pool. Instantly he stopped singing. Now that was a signal. When he stopped singing, his nearest neighbor stopped singing, then the next one and the next, and in a minute there wasn't a sound from the Smiling Pool save the squeak of Jerry Muskrat hidden among the bulrushes. That great chorus stopped as abruptly as the electric lights go out when you press a button.

Back and forth over the Smiling Pool, this way and that way, floated the shadow, but there was no sign of any living thing in the Smiling Pool. After awhile the shadow floated away over the Green Meadows without a sound.

"Hooty the Owl didn't get one of us that time," said Old Mr. Toad to his nearest neighbor with a chuckle of satisfaction. Then he swelled out his music bag and began to sing again. And at once, as abruptly as it had stopped, the great chorus began again as joyous as before, for nothing had happened to bring sadness as might have but for the watchfulness of Old Mr. Toad.

VIII

OLD MR. TOAD'S BABIES

The Smiling Pool's a nursery
　Where all the sunny day
A thousand funny babies
　Are taught while at their play.

Really the Smiling Pool is a sort of kindergarten, one of the most interesting kindergartens in the world. Little Joe Otter's children learn to swim there. So do Jerry Muskrat's babies and those of Billy Mink, the Trout and Minnow babies, and a lot more. And there you will find the children and grandchildren of Grandfather Frog and Old Mr. Toad.

Peter Rabbit had known for a long

time about the Frog babies, but though he knew that Old Mr. Toad was own cousin to Grandfather Frog, he hadn't known anything about Toad babies, except that at a certain time in the year he was forever running across tiny Toads, especially on rainy days, and each little Toad was just like Old Mr. Toad, except for his size. Peter had heard it said that Toads rain down from the sky, and sometimes it seems as if this must be so. Of course he knew it couldn't be, but it puzzled him a great deal. There wouldn't be a Toad in sight. Then it would begin to rain, and right away there would be so many tiny Toads that it was hard work to jump without stepping on some.

He remembered this as he went to pay his daily call on Old Mr. Toad in the Smiling Pool and listen to his sweet song. He hadn't seen any little Toads this year, but he remembered his experiences with them in other years, and he meant to ask about them.

Old Mr. Toad was sitting in his usual place, but he wasn't singing. He was staring at something in the water. When Peter said "Good Morning," Old Mr. Toad didn't seem to hear him. He was too much interested in what he was watching. Peter stared down into the water to see what was interesting Old Mr. Toad so much, but he saw nothing but a lot of wriggling tadpoles.

"What are you staring at so, Mr. Sobersides?" asked Peter, speaking a little louder than before.

Old Mr. Toad turned and looked at Peter, and there was a look of great pride in his face. "I'm just watching my babies. Aren't they lovely?" said he.

Peter stared harder than ever, but he couldn't see anything that looked like a baby Toad.

"Where are they?" asked he. "I don't see any babies but those of Grandfather Frog, and if you ask me, I always did think tadpoles about the homeliest things in the world."

Old Mr. Toad grew indignant. "Those are not Grandfather Frog's children; they're mine!" he sputtered. "And I'll have you know that they are the most beautiful babies in the world!"

Peter drew a hand across his mouth to hide a smile. "I beg your pardon, Mr. Toad," said he. "I—I thought all tadpoles were Frog babies. They all look alike to me."

"Well, they're not," declared Old Mr. Toad. "How anyone can mistake my babies for their cousins I cannot understand. Now mine are beautiful, while—"

"Chug-arum!" interrupted the great deep voice of Grandfather Frog. "What are you talking about? Why, your babies

38

are no more to be compared with my babies for real beauty than nothing at all! I'll leave it to Peter if they are."

But Peter wisely held his tongue. To tell the truth, he couldn't see beauty in any of them. To him they were all just wriggling pollywogs. They were more interesting now, because he had found out that some of them were Toads and some were Frogs, and he hadn't known before that baby Toads begin life as tadpoles, but he had no intention of being drawn into the dispute now waxing furious between Grandfather Frog and Old Mr. Toad.

IX

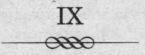

The Smiling Pool Kindergarten

Play a little, learn a little, grow a little too;
That's what every pollywoggy tries his best to
do.

Of course. That's what a kindergarten is for. And you may be sure that the babies of Grandfather Frog and Old Mr. Toad and Sticky-toes the Tree Toad did all of these things in the kindergarten of the Smiling Pool. They looked considerably alike, did these little cousins, for they were all pollywogs to begin with. Peter Rabbit came over every day to watch them. Always he had thought pollywogs just homely, wriggling things, not the least bit interesting, but since he had discovered how proud of them were Grandfather Frog and Old Mr. Toad, he had begun to wonder about them and then to watch them.

"There's one thing about them, and that is they are not in danger the way my babies are," said Peter, talking to himself as is his way when there is no one else to talk to. Just then a funny little black pollywog wriggled into sight, and while Peter was watching him, a stout-jawed water-beetle suddenly rushed from among the water grass, seized the pollywog by his tail, and dragged him down. Peter stared. Could it be that that ugly-looking bug was as dangerous an enemy to the baby Toad as Reddy Fox is to a baby Rabbit? He began to suspect so, and a little later he knew so, for there was that

41

same little pollywog trying hard to swim and making bad work of it, because he had lost half of his long tail.

That set Peter to watching sharper than ever, and presently he discovered that pollywogs have to keep their eyes open quite as much as do baby Rabbits, if they would live to grow up. There were several kinds of queer, ugly-looking bugs forever darting out at the wriggling pollywogs. Hungry-looking fish lay in wait for them, and Longlegs the Blue Heron seemed to have a special liking for them. But the pollywogs were spry, and seemed to have learned to watch out. They seemed to Peter to spend all their time swimming and eating and growing. They grew so fast that it seemed to him that he could almost *see* them grow. And just imagine how surprised Peter was to discover one day that that very pollywog which he had seen lose his tail had grown a *new* one. That puzzled Peter more than anything he had seen in a long time.

"Why, I couldn't do that!" he exclaimed right out loud.

"Do what?" demanded Jerry Muskrat, who happened along just then.

"Why, grow a new tail like that pollywog," replied Peter, and told Jerry all that he had seen. Jerry laughed.

"You'll see queerer things than that if you watch these pollywogs long enough," said he. "They are a queer lot of babies, and very interesting to watch if you've got the time for it. I haven't. This Smiling Pool is a great kindergarten, and there's something happening here every minute. There's no place like it."

"Are those great big fat pollywogs

Grandfather Frog's children, or Old Mr. Toad's?" asked Peter.

"Grandfather Frog's last year's children," replied Jerry. "They'll grow into real Frogs this summer, if nothing happens to them."

"Where are Old Mr. Toad's last year's children?" asked Peter.

"Don't ask me," replied Jerry. "They hopped away last summer. Never saw anything like the way those Toad youngsters grow. Those Toad pollywogs you see now will turn into real Toads, and be leaving the Smiling Pool in a few weeks. People think Old Mr. Toad is slow, but there is nothing slow about his children. Look at that little fellow over there; he's begun to grow legs already."

Peter looked, and sure enough there was a pollywog with a pair of legs sprouting out. They were his forelegs, and they certainly did make him look funny. And only a few days before there hadn't been a sign of legs.

"My gracious!" exclaimed Peter. "What a funny sight! I thought my babies grew fast, but these beat them."

X

THE LITTLE TOADS START OUT TO SEE THE WORLD

The world is a wonderful great big place
    And in it the young must roam
To learn what their elders have long since
    learned—
    There's never a place like home.

It had been some time since Peter Rabbit had visited the Smiling Pool to watch the pollywogs. But one cloudy morning he happened to think of them, and decided that he would run over there and see how they were getting along. So off he started, lipperty-lipperty-lip. He wondered if those pollywog children of Old Mr. Toad would be much changed. The last time he saw them some of them had just begun to grow legs, although they still had long tails.

He had almost reached the Smiling Pool when great big drops of rain began to splash down. And with those first raindrops something funny happened. Anyway, it seemed funny to Peter. Right away he was surrounded by tiny little Toads. Everywhere he looked he saw Toads, tiny little Toads just like Old Mr. Toad, only so tiny that one could have sat comfortably on a ten-cent piece and still had plenty of room.

Peter's big eyes grew round with surprise as he stared. Where had they all come from so suddenly? A minute before he hadn't seen a single one, and now he could hardly move without stepping on one. It seemed, it really seemed, as if each raindrop turned into a tiny Toad the instant it struck the ground. Of course Peter knew that that couldn't be, but it was very puzzling. And all those little Toads were bravely hopping along as if they were bound for some particular place.

Peter watched them for a few minutes, then he once more started for the Smiling Pool. On the very bank whom should he meet but Old Mr. Toad. He looked rather thin, and his back was to the Smiling Pool. Yes, Sir, he was hopping away from the Smiling Pool where he had been all the spring, singing in the great chorus. Peter was almost as surprised to see him as he had been to see the little Toads, but just then he was most interested in those little Toads.

"Good morning, Old Mr. Toad," said Peter in his most polite manner. "Can you tell me where all these little Toads came from?"

"Certainly," replied Old Mr. Toad. "They came from the Smiling Pool, of course. Where did you suppose they came from?"

"I—I didn't know. There wasn't one to be seen, and then it began to rain, and right away they were everywhere. It—it almost seemed as if they had rained down out of the sky."

Old Mr. Toad chuckled. "They've got good sense, if I must say it about my own children," said he. "They know that wet weather is the only weather for Toads to travel in. They left the Smiling Pool in the night while it was damp and comfortable, and then, when the sun came up, they hid, like sensible children, under anything they could find, sticks, stones, pieces of bark, grass. The minute this shower came up, they knew it was good traveling weather and out they popped."

"But what did they leave the Smiling Pool for?" Peter asked.

"To see the Great World," replied Old Mr. Toad. "Foolish, very foolish of them, but they would do it. I did the same thing myself when I was their age. Couldn't stop me any more than I could stop them. They don't know when they're well off, but young folks never do. Fine weather, isn't it?"

XI

~~~~~~

Old Mr. Toad's Queer Tongue

Old Mother Nature doth provide
　For all her children, large or small.
Her wisdom foresees all their needs
　And makes provision for them all.

If you don't believe it, just you go ask
Old Mr. Toad, as Peter Rabbit did,
how such a slow-moving fellow as he
is can catch enough bugs and insects to
keep him alive. Perhaps you'll learn
something just as Peter did. Peter and
Old Mr. Toad sat in the rain watching
the tiny Toads, who, you know, were Mr.
Toad's children, leaving their kindergarten in the Smiling Pool and starting out
to see the Great World. When the last

little Toad had passed them, Old Mr. Toad suddenly remembered that he was hungry, very hungry indeed.

"Didn't have time to eat much while I was in the Smiling Pool," he explained. "Couldn't eat and sing too, and while I was down there, I was supposed to sing. Now that it is time to quit singing, I begin to realize that I've got a stomach to look out for as well as a voice. See that bug over there on that leaf? Watch him."

Peter looked, and sure enough there was a fat bug crawling along on an old leaf. He was about two inches from Old Mr. Toad, and he was crawling very fast. And right while Peter was looking at him he disappeared. Peter turned to look at Old Mr. Toad. He hadn't budged. He was sitting exactly where he had been sitting all the time, but he was smacking his lips, and there was a twinkle of satisfaction in his eyes. Peter opened his eyes very wide.

"Wha—what—" he began.

"Nice bug," interrupted Old Mr. Toad. "Nicest bug I've eaten for a long time."

"But I didn't see you catch him!" protested Peter, looking at Old Mr. Toad as if he suspected him of joking.

"Anything wrong with your eyes?" inquired Old Mr. Toad.

"No," replied Peter just a wee bit crossly. "My eyes are just as good as ever."

"Then watch me catch that fly over yonder," said Old Mr. Toad. He hopped towards a fly which had lighted on a blade of grass just ahead. About two inches from it he stopped, and so far as Peter could see, he sat perfectly still. But the fly disappeared, and it wasn't because it flew away, either. Peter was sure of that. As he told Mrs. Peter about it afterwards, "It was there, and then it wasn't, and that was all there was to it."

Old Mr. Toad chuckled. "Didn't you see that one go, Peter?" he asked.

Peter shook his head. "I wish you would stop fooling me," said Peter. "The joke is on me, but now you've had your laugh at my expense, I wish you would tell me how you do it. Please, Mr. Toad."

Now when Peter said please that way, of course Old Mr. Toad couldn't resist him. Nobody could.

"Here comes an ant this way. Now you watch my mouth instead of the ant and see what happens," said Old Mr. Toad.

Peter looked and saw a big black ant coming. Then he kept his eyes on Old Mr. Toad's mouth. Suddenly there was a little flash of red from it, so tiny and so quick that Peter couldn't be absolutely sure that he saw it. But when he looked for the ant, it was nowhere to be seen. Peter looked at Old Mr. Toad very hard.

"Do you mean to tell me, Mr. Toad, that you've got a tongue long enough to reach way over to where that ant was?" he asked.

Old Mr. Toad chuckled again. With every insect swallowed he felt better natured. "You've guessed it, Peter," said he. "Handy tongue, isn't it?"

"I think it's a very queer tongue," retorted Peter, "and I don't understand it at all. If it's so long as all that, where do you keep it when it isn't in use? I should think you'd have to swallow it to get it out of the way, or else leave it hanging out of your mouth."

"Ha, ha, ha, ha, ha!" laughed Old Mr. Toad. "My tongue never is in the way, and it's the handiest tongue in the world. I'll show it to you."

XII

OLD MR. TOAD SHOWS HIS TONGUE

To show one's tongue, as you well know,
  Is not considered nice to do;
But if it were like Mr. Toad's
  I'd want to show it—wouldn't you?

I'm quite sure you would. You see, if it were like Old Mr. Toad's, it would be such a wonderful tongue that I suspect you would want everybody to see it. Old Mr. Toad thinks his tongue the most satisfactory tongue in the world. In fact, he is quite sure that without it he couldn't get along at all, and I don't know as he could. And yet very few of his neighbors know anything about that tongue and how different it is from most other tongues. Peter Rabbit didn't until Old Mr. Toad showed him after Peter had puzzled and puzzled over the mysterious way in which bugs and flies disappeared whenever they happened to come within two inches or less of Old Mr. Toad.

What Peter couldn't understand was what Old Mr. Toad did with a tongue that would reach two inches beyond his mouth. He said as much.

"I'll show you my tongue, and then you'll wish you had one just like it," said Old Mr. Toad, with a twinkle in his eyes.

He opened his big mouth and slowly ran his tongue out its full length. "Why! Why-ee!" exclaimed Peter. "It's fastened at the wrong end!"

"No such thing!" replied Old Mr. Toad indignantly. "If it was fastened at the other end, how could I run it out so far?"

"But mine and all other tongues that I

ever have seen are fastened way down in the throat," protested Peter. "Yours is fastened at the other end, way in the very front of your mouth. I never heard of such a thing."

"There are a great many things you have never heard of, Peter Rabbit," replied Old Mr. Toad drily. "Mine is the right way to have a tongue. Because it is fastened way up in the front of my mouth that way, I can use the whole of it. You see it goes out its full length. Then, when I draw it in with a bug on the end of it, I just turn it over so that the end that was out goes way back in my throat and takes the bug with it to just the right place to swallow."

Peter thought this over for a few minutes before he ventured another question. "I begin to understand," said he, "but how do you hold on to the bug with your tongue?"

58

"My tongue is sticky, of course, Mr. Stupid," replied Old Mr. Toad, looking very much disgusted. "Just let me touch a bug with it, and he's mine every time."

Peter thought this over. Then he felt of his own tongue. "Mine isn't sticky," said he very innocently.

Old Mr. Toad laughed right out. "Perhaps if it was, you couldn't ask so many questions," said he. "Now watch me catch that fly." His funny little tongue darted out, and the fly was gone.

"It certainly is very handy," said Peter politely. "I think we are going to have more rain, and I'd better be getting back to the dear Old Briar-patch. Very much obliged to you, Mr. Toad. I think you are very wonderful."

"Not at all," replied Old Mr. Toad. "I've simply got the things I need in order to live, just as you have the things you need. I couldn't get along with your kind of tongue, but no more could you get along with mine. If you live long enough, you will learn that Old Mother Nature makes no mistakes. She gives each of us what we need, and each one has different needs."

XIII

PETER RABBIT IS IMPOLITE

Peter Rabbit couldn't get Old Mr. Toad off his mind. He had discovered so many interesting things about Old Mr. Toad that he was almost on the point of believing him to be the most interesting of all his neighbors. And his respect for Old Mr. Toad had become very great indeed. Of course. Who wouldn't respect anyone with such beautiful eyes and such a sweet voice and such a wonderful tongue? Yet at the same time Peter felt very foolish whenever he remembered that all his life he had been acquainted with Old Mr. Toad without really knowing him at all. There was one comforting thought, and that was that most of his neighbors were just as ignorant regarding Old Mr. Toad as Peter had been.

"Funny," mused Peter, "how we can live right beside people all our lives and not really know them at all. I suppose that is why we should never judge people hastily. I believe I will go hunt up Old Mr. Toad and see if I can find out anything more."

Off started Peter, lipperty-lipperty-lip. He didn't know just where to go, now that Old Mr. Toad had left the Smiling Pool, but he had an idea that he would not be far from their meeting place of the day before, when Old Mr. Toad had explained about his wonderful tongue. But when he got there, Peter found no trace of Old Mr. Toad. You see, it had rained the day before, and that is just the kind of weather that a Toad likes best for traveling. Peter ought to have thought of that, but he didn't. He hunted for awhile and finally gave it up and started up the Crooked Little Path with the idea of running over for a call on Johnny Chuck in the Old Orchard.

Jolly, round, bright Mr. Sun was shining his brightest, and Peter soon forgot all about Old Mr. Toad. He scampered along up the Crooked Little Path, thinking of nothing in particular but how good it was to be alive, and occasionally kicking up his heels for pure joy. He had just done this when his ears caught the sound of a queer noise a little to one side of the Crooked Little Path. Instantly Peter stopped and sat up to listen. There it was again, and it seemed to come from under an old piece of board. It was just a little, rustling sound, hardly to be heard.

"There's someone under that old board," thought Peter, and peeped under.

All he could see was that there was
something moving. Instantly Peter was
all curiosity. Whoever was there was not
very big. He was sure of that. Of course
that meant that he had nothing to fear.
So what do you think Peter did? Why, he
just pulled that old board over. And
when he did that, he saw, whom do you
think? Why, Old Mr. Toad, to be sure.

But such a sight as Old Mr. Toad was!
Peter just stared. For a full minute he
couldn't find his voice. Old Mr. Toad was
changing his clothes! Yes, Sir, that is
just what Old Mr. Toad was doing. He
was taking off his old suit, and under it
was a brand new one. But such a time as
he was having! He was opening and
shutting his big mouth, and drawing his
hind legs under him, and rubbing them
against his body. Then Peter saw a
strange thing. He saw that Old Mr.

Toad's old suit had split in several places, and he was getting it off by sucking it into his mouth!

In a few minutes his hind legs were free of the old suit, and little by little it began to be pulled free from his body. All the time Old Mr. Toad was working very hard to suck it at the corners of his big mouth. He glared angrily at Peter, but he couldn't say anything because his mouth was too full. He looked so funny that Peter just threw himself on the ground and rolled over and over with laughter. This made Old Mr. Toad glare more angrily than ever, but he couldn't say anything, not a word.

When he had got his hands free by pulling the sleeves of his old coat off inside out, he used his hands to pull the last of it over his head. Then he gulped very hard two or three times to swallow

his old suit, and when the last of it had disappeared, he found his voice.

"Don't you know that it is the most impolite thing in the world to look at people when they are changing their clothes?" he sputtered.

XIV

Old Mr. Toad Disappears

Admit your fault when you've done wrong,
  And don't postpone it over long.

Peter Rabbit didn't blame Old Mr.
Toad a bit for being indignant because Peter had watched him
change his suit. It wasn't a nice thing to
do. Old Mr. Toad had looked very funny
while he was struggling out of his old
suit, and Peter just couldn't help laughing at him. But he realized that he had
been very impolite, and he very meekly
told Old Mr. Toad so.

"You see, it was this way," explained
Peter. "I heard something under that old

board, and I just naturally turned it over to find out what was there."

"Hump!" grunted Old Mr. Toad.

"I didn't have the least idea that you were there," continued Peter. "When I found who it was, and what you were doing, I couldn't help watching because it was so interesting, and I couldn't help laughing because you really did look so funny. But I'm sorry, Mr. Toad. Truly I am. I didn't mean to be so impolite. I promise never to do it again. I don't suppose, Mr. Toad, that it seems at all wonderful to you that you can change your suit that way, but it does to me. I had heard that you swallowed your old suits, but I never half believed it. Now I know it is so and just how you do it, and I feel as if I had learned something worth knowing. Do you know, I think you are one of the most interesting and wonderful of all my neighbors, and I'll never laugh at or tease you again, Mr. Toad."

"Hump!" grunted Old Mr. Toad again, but it was very clear that he was a little flattered by Peter's interest in him and was rapidly recovering his good nature.

"There is one thing I don't understand yet," said Peter, "and that is where you go to sleep all winter. Do you go down into the mud at the bottom of the Smiling Pool the way Grandfather Frog does?"

"Certainly not!" retorted Old Mr. Toad. "Use your common sense, Peter Rabbit. If I had spent the winter in the Smiling Pool, do you suppose I would have left it to come way up here and then have turned right around and gone back there to sing? I'm not so fond of long journeys as all that."

"That's so." Peter looked foolish. "I didn't think of that when I spoke."

"The trouble with you, and with a lot of other people, is that you speak first and do your thinking afterward, when you do any thinking at all," grunted Old Mr. Toad. "Now if I wanted to, I could disappear right here."

"You mean that you would hide under that old board just as you did before," said Peter, with a very wise look.

"Nothing of the sort!" snapped Old Mr. Toad. "I could disappear and not go near that old board, not a step nearer than I am now."

Peter looked in all directions carefully, but not a thing could he see under which Old Mr. Toad could possibly hide except the old board, and he had said he wouldn't hide under that. "I don't like to doubt your word, Mr. Toad," said he, "but you'll have to show me before I can believe that."

Old Mr. Toad's eyes twinkled. Here was a chance to get even with Peter for watching him change his suit. "If you'll turn your back to me and look straight down the Crooked Little Path for five minutes, I'll disappear," said he. "More than that, I give you my word of honor that I will not hop three feet from where I am sitting."

"All right," replied Peter promptly, turning his back to Old Mr. Toad. "I'll look down the Crooked Little Path for five minutes and promise not to peek."

So Peter sat and gazed straight down the Crooked Little Path. It was a great temptation to roll his eyes back and peep behind him, but he had given his word that he wouldn't, and he didn't. When he thought the five minutes were up, he

turned around. Old Mr. Toad was nowhere to be seen. Peter looked hastily
this way and that way, but there was not
a sign of Old Mr. Toad. He had disappeared as completely as if he never had
been there.

XV

OLD MR. TOAD GIVES PETER A SCARE

If you play pranks on other folks
  You may be sure that they
Will take the first chance that they get
  A joke on you to play.

Old Mr. Toad was getting even with Peter for laughing at him. While Peter's back had been turned, Old Mr. Toad had disappeared.

It was too much for Peter. Look as he would, he couldn't see so much as a chip under which Old Mr. Toad might have hidden, excepting the old board, and Old Mr. Toad had given his word of honor that he wouldn't hide under that. Nevertheless, Peter hopped over to it and turned it over again, because he couldn't think of any other place to look. Of course, Old Mr. Toad wasn't there. Of course not. He had given his word that he wouldn't hide there, and he always lives up to his word. Peter should have known better than to have looked there.

Old Mr. Toad had also said that he would not go three feet from the spot where he was sitting at the time, so Peter should have known better than to have raced up the Crooked Little Path as he did. But if Old Mr. Toad had nothing to hide under, of course he must have hopped away, reasoned Peter. He couldn't hop far in five minutes, that was sure, and so Peter ran this way and that way a great deal farther than it would have been possible for Old Mr. Toad to have gone. But it was a wholly useless search, and presently Peter returned and sat down on the very spot

where he had last seen Old Mr. Toad.
Peter never had felt more foolish in all
his life. He began to think that Old Mr.
Toad must be bewitched and had some
strange power of making himself invisi-
ble.

For a long time Peter sat perfectly
still, trying to puzzle out how Old Mr.
Toad had disappeared, but the more he
puzzled over it, the more impossible it
seemed. And yet Old Mr. Toad had disappeared. Suddenly Peter gave a frightened scream and jumped higher than he
ever had jumped before in all his life. A
voice, the voice of Old Mr. Toad himself,
had said, "Well, now are you satisfied?"
*And that voice had come from right
under Peter!* Do you wonder that he was
frightened? When he turned to look,
there sat Old Mr. Toad right where he
himself had been sitting a moment be-

fore. Peter rubbed his eyes and stared very foolishly.

"Wh-wh-where did you come from?" he stammered at last.

Old Mr. Toad grinned. "I'll show you," said he. And right while Peter was looking at him, he began to sink down into the ground until only the top of his head could be seen. Then that disappeared. Old Mr. Toad had gone down, and the sand had fallen right back over him. Peter just had to rub his eyes again. He had to! Then, to make sure, he began to dig away the sand where Old Mr. Toad had been sitting. In a minute he felt Old Mr. Toad, who at once came out again.

Old Mr. Toad's beautiful eyes twinkled more than ever. "I guess we are even now, Peter," said he.

Peter nodded. "More than that, Mr. Toad. I think you have a little the best of it," he replied. "Now won't you tell me how you did it?"

Old Mr. Toad held up one of his stout hind feet, and on it was a kind of spur. "There's another just like that on the other foot," said he, "and I use them to dig with. You go into a hole head-first, but I go in the other way. I make my hole in the soft earth and back into it at the same time, this way." He began to work his stout hind feet, and as he kicked the earth out, he backed in at the same time. When he was deep enough, the earth just fell back over him, for you see it was very loose and not packed down at all. When he once more reappeared, Peter thanked him. Then he asked one more question.

"Is that the way you go into winter quarters?"

Old Mr. Toad nodded. "And it's the way I escape from my enemies."

XVI

Jimmy Skunk Is Surprised

Jimmy Skunk ambled along the Crooked Little Path down the hill. He didn't hurry because Jimmy doesn't believe in hurrying. The only time he ever hurries is when he sees a fat beetle trying to get out of sight. Then Jimmy *does* hurry. But just now he didn't see any fat beetles, although he was looking for them. So he just ambled along as if he had all the time in the world, as indeed he had. He was feeling very good-natured, was Jimmy Skunk. And why shouldn't he? There was everything to make him feel good-natured. Summer had arrived to stay. On every side he heard glad voices. Bumble the

Bee was humming a song. Best of all, Jimmy had found three beetles that very morning, and he knew that there were more if he could find them. So why shouldn't he feel good?

Jimmy had laughed at Peter Rabbit for being so anxious for Summer to arrive, but he was just as glad as Peter that she had come, although he wouldn't have said so for the world. His sharp little eyes twinkled as he ambled along, and there wasn't much that they missed. As he walked he talked, quite to himself of course, because there was nobody near to hear, and this is what he was saying:

> "Beetle, beetle, smooth and smug,
>   You are nothing but a bug.
> Bugs were made for Skunks to eat,
>   So come out from your retreat.

"Hello! There's a nice big piece of bark over there that looks as if it ought to have a dozen fat beetles under it. It's great fun to pull over pieces of bark and see fat beetles run all ways at once. I'll just have to see what is under that piece."

Jimmy tiptoed softly over to the big piece of bark, and then as he made ready to turn it over, he began again that foolish little verse.

"Beetle, beetle, smooth and smug,
    You are nothing but a bug."

As he said the last word, he suddenly pulled the piece of bark over.

"Who's a bug?" asked a funny voice, and it sounded rather cross. Jimmy Skunk nearly tumbled over backward in surprise, and for a minute he couldn't find his tongue. There, instead of the fat

beetles he had been so sure of, sat Old Mr. Toad, and he didn't look at all pleased.

"Who's a bug?" he repeated.

Instead of answering, Jimmy Skunk began to laugh. "Who's a bug?" demanded Old Mr. Toad, more crossly than before.

"There isn't any bug, Mr. Toad, and I beg your pardon," replied Jimmy, remembering his politeness. "I just thought there was. You see, I didn't know you were under that piece of bark. I hope you will excuse me, Mr. Toad. Have you seen any fat beetles this morning?"

"No," said Old Mr. Toad grumpily, and yawned and rubbed his eyes.

"Why," exclaimed Jimmy Skunk, "I believe you have just waked up!"

"What if I have?" demanded Old Mr. Toad.

"Oh, nothing, nothing at all, Mr. Toad," replied Jimmy Skunk, "only you are the second one I've met this morning who had just waked up."

"Who was the other?" asked Old Mr. Toad.

"Mr. Blacksnake," replied Jimmy. "He inquired for you."

Old Mr. Toad turned quite pale. "I—I think I'll be moving along," said he.

XVII

OLD MR. TOAD'S MISTAKE

I f" is a very little word to look at, but the biggest word you have ever seen doesn't begin to have so much meaning as little "if." *If* Jimmy Skunk hadn't ambled down the Crooked Little Path just when he did; *if* he hadn't been looking for fat beetles; *if* he hadn't seen that big piece of bark at one side and decided to pull it over; *if* it hadn't been for all these "ifs," why Old Mr. Toad wouldn't have made the mistake he did, and you wouldn't have had this story. But Jimmy Skunk *did* amble down the Crooked Little Path, he *did* look for beetles, and he *did* pull over that big piece of bark. And

when he had pulled it over, he found Old
Mr. Toad there.

Old Mr. Toad had crept under that
piece of bark because he wanted to take
a nap. But when Jimmy Skunk told him
that he had seen Mr. Blacksnake that
very morning, and that Mr. Blacksnake
had asked after Old Mr. Toad, the very
last bit of sleepiness left Old Mr. Toad.
Yes, Sir, he was wide awake right away.
You see, he knew right away why Mr.
Blacksnake had asked after him. He
knew that Mr. Blacksnake has a fond-
ness for Toads. He turned quite pale
when he heard that Mr. Blacksnake had
asked after him, and right then he made
his mistake. He was in such a hurry to
get away from that neighborhood that
he forgot to ask Jimmy Skunk just
where he had seen Mr. Blacksnake. He
hardly waited long enough to say

good-by to Jimmy Skunk, but started off as fast as he could go.

Now it just happened that Old Mr. Toad started up the Crooked Little Path, and it just happened that Mr. Black-snake was coming down the Crooked Little Path. Now when people are very much afraid, they almost always seem to think that danger is behind instead of in front of them. It was so with Old Mr. Toad. Instead of watching out in front as he hopped along, he kept watching over his shoulder, and that was his second mistake. He was so sure that Mr. Black-snake was somewhere behind him that he didn't look to see where he was going, and you know that people who don't look to see where they are going are almost sure to go headfirst right into trouble.

Old Mr. Toad went hopping up the Crooked Little Path as fast as he could, which wasn't very fast because he never can hop very fast. And all the time he kept looking behind for Mr. Blacksnake. Presently he came to a turn in the Crooked Little Path, and as he hurried around it, he almost ran into Mr. Blacksnake himself. It was a question which was more surprised. For just a wee second they stared at each other. Then Mr. Blacksnake's eyes began to sparkle.

"Good morning, Mr. Toad. Isn't this a beautiful morning? I was just thinking about you," said he.

But poor Old Mr. Toad didn't say good morning. He didn't say anything. He couldn't, because he was too scared. He just gave a frightened little squeal, turned around, and started down the Crooked Little Path twice as fast as he had come up. Mr. Blacksnake grinned and started after him, not very fast because he knew that he wouldn't have to run very fast to catch Old Mr. Toad, and he thought the exercise would do him good.

And this is how it happened that summer morning that jolly, bright Mr. Sun, looking down from the blue, blue sky and smiling to see how happy everybody seemed, suddenly discovered that there was one of the little meadow people who wasn't happy, but instead was terribly, terribly unhappy. It was Old Mr. Toad hopping down the Crooked Little Path for his life, while after him, and getting nearer and nearer, glided Mr. Blacksnake.

XVIII

JIMMY SKUNK IS JUST IN TIME

Jimmy Skunk ambled slowly along, chuckling as he thought of what a hurry Mr. Toad had been in, when he had heard that Mr. Blacksnake had asked after him. It had been funny, very funny indeed, to see Mr. Toad try to hurry.

Suddenly Jimmy stopped chuckling. Then he stopped ambling along the Crooked Little Path. He turned around and looked back, and as he did so he scratched his head thoughtfully. He had just happened to think that Old Mr. Toad had gone up the Crooked Little Path, and it was *up* the Crooked Little Path that

Mr. Blacksnake had shown himself that morning.

"If he's still up there," thought Jimmy, "Old Mr. Toad is hopping right straight into the very worst kind of trouble. How stupid of him not to have asked me where Mr. Blacksnake was! Well, it's none of my business. I guess I'll go on."

But he had gone on down the Crooked Little Path only a few steps when he stopped again. You see, Jimmy is really a very kind-hearted little fellow, and somehow he didn't like to think of what might happen to Old Mr. Toad.

"I hate to go way back there," he grumbled, for you know he is naturally rather lazy. "Still, the Green Meadows wouldn't be quite the same without Old Mr. Toad. I should miss him if anything happened to him. I suppose it would be partly my fault, too, for if I hadn't pulled over that piece of bark, he probably would have stayed there the rest of the day and been safe."

"Maybe he won't meet Mr. Black-snake," said a little voice inside of Jimmy.

"And maybe he will," said Jimmy right out loud. And with that, he started back up the Crooked Little Path, and strange to say Jimmy hurried.

He had just reached a turn in the Crooked Little Path when who should run right plump into him but poor Old Mr. Toad. He gave a frightened squeal and fell right over on his back, and kicked foolishly as he tried to get on his feet again. But he was all out of breath, and so frightened and tired that all he could do was to kick and kick. He hadn't seen Jimmy at all, for he had been look-ing behind him, and he didn't even know who it was he had run into.

Right behind him came Mr. Blacksnake. Of course he saw Jimmy, and he stopped short and hissed angrily.

"What were you going to do to Mr. Toad?" demanded Jimmy.

"None of your business!" hissed Mr. Blacksnake. "Get out of my way, or you'll be sorry."

Jimmy Skunk just laughed and stepped in front of poor Old Mr. Toad. Mr. Blacksnake coiled himself up in the path and darted his tongue out at Jimmy in the most impudent way. Then he tried to make himself look very fierce. Then he jumped straight at Jimmy Skunk with his mouth wide open, but he took great care not to jump quite far enough to reach Jimmy. You see, he was just trying to scare Jimmy. But Jimmy didn't scare. He knows all about Mr. Blacksnake and that really he is a coward. So he suddenly gritted his teeth in a way not at all pleasant to hear and started for Mr. Blacksnake. Mr. Black-snake didn't wait. No, Sir, he didn't wait. He suddenly turned and glided back up the Crooked Little Path, hissing angrily. Jimmy followed him a little way, and then he went back to Old Mr. Toad.

"Oh," panted Mr. Toad, "you came just in time! I couldn't have hopped another hop."

"I guess I did," replied Jimmy. "Now you get your breath and come along with me." And Old Mr. Toad did.

XIX

Old Mr. Toad Gets His Stomach Full

Pray do not tip your nose in scorn
  At things which others eat,
For things to you not good at all
  To others are most sweet.

There are ants, for instance. You wouldn't want to eat them even if you were dreadfully hungry. But Old Mr. Toad and Buster Bear think there is nothing much nicer. Now Buster Bear had found Old Mr. Toad catching ants, one at a time, as he kept watch beside their home, and it had pleased Buster to find someone else who liked ants. Right away he invited Old Mr. Toad to dine with him. But poor Old Mr. Toad was frightened almost to death when he heard the deep, grumbly-rumbly voice of Buster Bear, for he had been so busy watching the ants that he hadn't seen Buster coming.

He fell right over on his back, which wasn't at all dignified, and made Buster Bear laugh. That frightened Mr. Toad more than ever. You see he didn't have the least doubt in the world that Buster Bear meant to eat him, and when Buster invited him to dinner, he was sure that that was just a joke on Buster's part.

But there was no way to escape, and after a little Old Mr. Toad thought it best to be polite, because, you know, it always pays to be polite. So he said in a very faint voice that he would be pleased to dine with Buster. Then he waved his feet feebly, trying to get on his feet again. Buster Bear laughed harder than ever. It was a low, deep, grumbly-rumbly laugh, and sent cold shivers all over poor Old Mr. Toad. But when Buster reached out a great paw with great cruel-looking claws Mr. Toad quite gave up. He didn't have strength enough left to even kick. He just closed his eyes and waited for the end.

What do you think happened? Why, he was rolled over on to his feet so gently that he just gasped with surprise. It didn't seem possible that such a great paw could be so gentle.

"Now," said Buster Bear in a voice which he tried to make sound pleasant, but which was grumbly-rumbly just the same, "I know where there is a fine dinner waiting for us just a little way from here. You follow me, and we'll have it in no time."

So Buster Bear led the way, and Old Mr. Toad followed as fast as he could, because he didn't dare not to. Presently

Buster stopped beside a big decayed old log. "If you are ready, Mr. Toad, we will dine now," said he.

Old Mr. Toad didn't see anything to eat. His heart sank again, and he shook all over. "I—I'm not hungry," said he in a very faint voice.

Buster Bear didn't seem to hear. He hooked his great claws into the old log and gave a mighty pull. Over rolled the log, and there were ants and ants and ants, hurrying this way and scurrying that way, more ants than Mr. Toad had seen in all his life before!

"Help yourself," said Buster Bear politely.

Old Mr. Toad didn't wait to be told twice. He forgot all about his fright. He forgot all about Buster Bear. He forgot that he wasn't hungry. He forgot his manners. He jumped right in among those ants, and for a little while he was the busiest Toad ever seen. Buster Bear was busy too. He swept his long tongue this way, and he swept it that way, and each time he drew it back into his mouth, it was covered with ants. At last Old Mr. Toad couldn't hold another ant. Then he remembered Buster Bear and looked up a little fearfully. Buster was smacking his lips, and there was a twinkle in each eye.

"Good, aren't they?" said he.

"The best I ever ate," declared Old Mr. Toad with a sigh of satisfaction.

"Come dine with me again," said Buster Bear, and somehow this time Old Mr. Toad didn't mind because his voice sounded grumbly-rumbly.

"Thank you, I will," replied Old Mr. Toad.

XX

OLD MR. TOAD IS PUFFED UP

Old Mr. Toad hopped slowly down the Lone Little Path. He usually does hop slowly, but this time he hopped slower than ever. You see, he was so puffed up that he couldn't have hopped fast if he had wanted to, and he didn't want to. In the first place his stomach was so full of ants that there wasn't room for another one. No, Sir, Old Mr. Toad couldn't have swallowed another ant if he had tried. Of course they made his stomach stick out, but it wasn't the ants that puffed him out all over. Oh, my, no! It was pride. That's what it was—pride. You know nothing can puff anyone up quite like foolish pride.

Old Mr. Toad was old enough to have known better. It is bad enough to see young and foolish creatures puffed up with pride, but it is worse to see anyone as old as Old Mr. Toad that way. He held his head so high that he couldn't see his own feet, and more than once he stubbed his toes. Presently he met his old friend, Danny Meadow Mouse. He tipped his head a little higher, puffed himself out a little more, and pretended not to see Danny.

"Hello, Mr. Toad," said Danny.

Mr. Toad pretended not to hear. Danny looked puzzled. Then he spoke again, and this time he shouted: "Hello, Mr. Toad! I haven't seen you for some time."

It wouldn't do to pretend not to hear this time. "Oh, how do you do, Danny?" said Old Mr. Toad with a very grand air,

and pretending to be much surprised. "Sorry I can't stop, but I've been dining with my friend, Buster Bear, and now I must get home." When he mentioned the name of Buster Bear, he puffed himself out a little more.

Danny grinned as he watched him hop on down the Lone Little Path. "Can't talk with common folks anymore," he muttered. "I've heard that pride is very apt to turn people's heads, but I never expected to see Old Mr. Toad proud."

Mr. Toad kept on his way, and presently he met Peter Rabbit. Peter stopped to gossip, as is his way. But Old Mr. Toad took no notice of him at all. He kept right on with his head high, and all puffed out. Peter might have been a stick or a stone for all the notice Old Mr. Toad took of him. Peter looked puzzled.

Then he hurried down to tell Danny Meadow Mouse about it.

"Oh," said Danny, "he's been to dine with Buster Bear, and now he has no use for his old friends."

Pretty soon along came Johnny Chuck, and he was very much put out because he had been treated by Old Mr. Toad just as Peter Rabbit had. Striped Chipmunk told the same story. So did Unc' Billy Possum. It was the same with all of Old Mr. Toad's old friends and neighbors, excepting Bobby Coon, who, you know, is Buster Bear's little cousin. To him Old Mr. Toad was very polite and talked a great deal about Buster Bear, and thought that Bobby must be very proud to be related to Buster.

At first everybody thought it a great joke to see Old Mr. Toad so puffed up with pride, but after a little they grew tired of being snubbed by their old friend

and neighbor, and began to say unpleasant things about him. Then they decided that what Old Mr. Toad needed was a lesson, so they put their heads together and planned how they would teach Old Mr. Toad how foolish it is for anyone to be puffed up with pride.

XXI

OLD MR. TOAD RECEIVES ANOTHER INVITATION

The friends and neighbors of Old Mr. Toad decided that he needed to be taught a lesson. At first, you know, everyone had laughed at him, because he had grown too proud to speak to them, but after a little they grew tired of being treated so, and some of them put their heads together to think of some plan to teach Old Mr. Toad a lesson and what a very, very foolish thing false pride is. The very next day Jimmy Skunk went into the Green Forest to look for Buster Bear. You know Jimmy isn't afraid of Buster. He didn't have to look long, and when he had found him, the very first thing he did was to ask

Buster if he had seen any fat beetles that morning. You know Jimmy is very fond of fat beetles, and the first thing he asks anyone he may happen to meet is if they have seen any.

Buster Bear grinned and said he thought he knew where there might be a few, and he would be pleased to have Jimmy go with him to see. Sure enough, under an old log he found five fat beetles, and these Jimmy gobbled up without even asking Buster if he would have one. Jimmy is usually very polite, but this time he quite forgot politeness. I am afraid he is rather apt to when fat beetles are concerned. But Buster didn't seem to mind. When the last beetle had disappeared Jimmy smacked his lips, and then he told Buster Bear what he had come for. Of course, at first Buster had thought it was for the fat beetles. But it wasn't. No, Sir, it wasn't for the

fat beetles at all. It was to get Buster
Bear's help in a plan to teach Old Mr.
Toad a lesson.

First Jimmy told Buster all about how
puffed up Old Mr. Toad was because he
had dined with Buster, and how ever
since then he had refused even to speak
to his old friends and neighbors. It tick-
led Buster Bear so to think that little
homely Old Mr. Toad could be proud of
anything that he laughed and laughed,
and his laugh was deep and grumbly-
rumbly. Then Jimmy told him the plan
to teach Old Mr. Toad a lesson and asked
Buster if he would help. Buster's eyes
twinkled as he promised to do what
Jimmy asked.

Then Jimmy went straight to where
Old Mr. Toad was sitting all puffed up,
taking a sun-bath.

"Buster Bear has just sent word by me
to ask if you will honor him by dining

with him to-morrow at the rotted chestnut stump near the edge of the Green
Forest," said Jimmy in his politest manner.

Now if Old Mr. Toad was puffed up before, just think how he swelled out when
he heard that. Jimmy Skunk was actually afraid that he would burst.

"You may tell my friend, Buster Bear,
that I shall be very happy to honor him
by dining with him," replied Old Mr.
Toad with a very grand air.

Jimmy went off to deliver his reply,
and Old Mr. Toad sat and puffed himself
out until he could hardly breathe. "Honor
him by dining with him," said he over
and over to himself. "I never was so flattered in my life."

XXII

OLD MR. TOAD LEARNS A LESSON

Pride is like a great big bubble;
　You'll find there's nothing in it.
Prick it and for all your trouble
　It has vanished in a minute.

Old Mr. Toad was so puffed out
with pride as he started for the
Green Forest to dine with Buster
Bear that those who saw him wondered
if he wouldn't burst before he got there.
Everybody knew where he was going,
and this made Old Mr. Toad feel more
important and proud than ever. He
might not have felt quite so puffed up if
he had known just how it had come
about that he received this second invi-

tation to dine with Buster Bear. When Jimmy Skunk brought it to him, Jimmy didn't tell him that Buster had been asked to send the invitation, and that it was all part of a plan on the part of some of Old Mr. Toad's old friends and neighbors to teach him a lesson. No, indeed, Jimmy didn't say anything at all about that!

So Old Mr. Toad went hopping along and stumbling over his own feet, because his head was held so high and he was so puffed out that he couldn't see where he was going. He could think of nothing but how important Buster Bear must consider him to invite him to dinner a second time, and of the delicious ants he was sure he would have to eat.

"What very good taste Buster Bear has," thought he, "and how very fortunate it is that he found out that I also am fond of ants."

He was so busy with these pleasant thoughts and of the good dinner that he expected to have that he took no notice of what was going on about him. He didn't see his old friends and neighbors peeping out at him and laughing because he looked so foolish and silly. He was dressed in his very best, which was nothing at all to be proud of, for you know Old Mr. Toad has no fine clothes. And being puffed up so, he was homelier than ever, which is saying a great deal, for at best Mr. Toad is anything but handsome.

He was beginning to get pretty tired by the time he reached the Green Forest and came in sight of the rotted old chestnut stump where he was to meet Buster Bear.

Buster was waiting for him. "How do you do this fine day? You look a little tired and rather warm, Mr. Toad," said he.

"I am a little warm," replied Mr. Toad in his most polite manner, although he couldn't help panting for breath as he said it. "I hope you are feeling as well as you are looking, Mr. Bear."

Buster Bear laughed a great, grumbly-rumbly laugh. "I always feel fine when there is a dinner of fat ants ready for me," said he. "It is fine of you to honor me by coming to dine."

Here Mr. Toad put one hand on his stomach and tried to make a very grand bow. Peter Rabbit, hiding behind a nearby tree, almost giggled aloud, he looked so funny.

"I have ventured to invite another to enjoy the dinner with us," continued

Buster Bear. Mr. Toad's face fell. You see he was selfish. He wanted to be the only one to have the honor of dining with Buster Bear. "He's a little late," went on Buster, "but I think he will be here soon, and I hope you will be glad to meet him. Ah, there he comes now!"

Old Mr. Toad looked in the direction in which Buster Bear was looking. He gave a little gasp and turned quite pale. All his puffiness disappeared. He didn't look like the same Toad at all. The new-comer was Mr. Blacksnake. "Oh!" cried Old Mr. Toad, and then, without even asking to be excused, he turned his back on Buster Bear and started back the way he had come, with long, frightened hops.

"Ha, ha, ha!" shouted Peter Rabbit, jumping out from behind a tree.

"Ho, ho, ho!" shouted Jimmy Skunk from behind another.

"Hee, hee, hee!" shouted Johnny Chuck from behind a third.

Then Old Mr. Toad knew that his old friends and neighbors had planned this to teach him a lesson.

XXIII

———⦻———

OLD MR. TOAD IS VERY HUMBLE

When Old Mr. Toad saw Mr. Blacksnake and turned his back on Buster Bear and the fine dinner to which Buster had invited him, he had but just one idea in his head, and that was to get out of sight of Mr. Blacksnake as soon as possible. He forgot to ask Buster Bear to excuse him. He forgot that he was tired and hot. He forgot all the pride with which he had been so puffed up. He forgot everything but the need of getting out of sight of Mr. Blacksnake as soon as ever he could. So away went Old Mr. Toad, hop, hop, hipperty-hop, hop, hop,

hipperty-hop! He heard Peter Rabbit
and Jimmy Skunk and Johnny Chuck
and others of his old friends and neighbors shouting with laughter. Yes, and
he heard the deep, grumbly-rumbly
laugh of Buster Bear. But he didn't
mind it. Not then, anyway. He hadn't
room for any feeling except fear of Mr.
Blacksnake.

But Old Mr. Toad had to stop after a
while. You see, his legs were so tired
they just wouldn't go any longer. And he
was so out of breath that he wheezed.
He crawled under a big piece of bark,
and there he lay flat on the ground and
panted and panted for breath. He would
stay there until jolly, round, bright Mr.
Sun went to bed behind the Purple Hills.
Then Mr. Blacksnake would go to bed
too, and it would be safe for him to go
home. Now, lying there in the dark, for it

was dark under that big piece of bark, Old Mr. Toad had time to think. Little by little he began to understand that his invitation to dine with Buster Bear had been part of a plan by his old friends and neighbors whom he had so snubbed and looked down on when he had been puffed up with pride, to teach him a lesson. At first he was angry, very angry indeed. Then he began to see how foolish and silly he had been, and shame took the place of anger. As he remembered the deep, grumbly-rumbly laughter of Buster Bear, the feeling of shame grew.

"I deserve it," thought Old Mr. Toad. "Yes, Sir, I deserve every bit of it. The only thing that I have to be proud of is that I'm honest and work for my living. Yes, Sir, that's all."

When darkness came at last, and he crawled out to go home, he was feeling very humble. Peter Rabbit happened along just then. Old Mr. Toad opened his mouth to speak, but Peter suddenly threw his head up very high and strutted past as if he didn't see Old Mr. Toad at all. Mr. Toad gulped and went on. Pretty soon he met Jimmy Skunk. Jimmy went right on about his business and actually stepped right over Old Mr. Toad as if he had been a stick or a stone. Old Mr. Toad gulped again and went on. The next day he went down to see Danny Meadow Mouse. He meant to tell Danny how ashamed he was for the way he had treated Danny and his other friends. But Danny brushed right past without even a glance at him. Old Mr. Toad gulped and started up to see Johnny Chuck. The same thing happened again. So it did when he met Striped Chipmunk.

At last Old Mr. Toad gave up and went home, where he sat under a big mullein leaf the rest of the day, feeling very miserable and lonely. He didn't have appetite enough to snap at a single fly. Late that afternoon he heard a little noise and looked up to find all his old friends and neighbors forming a circle around him. Suddenly they began to dance and shout:

"Old Mr. Toad is a jolly good fellow!
His temper is sweet, disposition is mellow!
And now that his bubble of pride is quite busted,
We know that he knows that his friends can be trusted."

Then Old Mr. Toad knew that all was well once more, and presently he began to dance too, the funniest dance that ever was seen.

That is all for now about homely Old

Mr. Toad, because I have just got to tell you about another homely fellow—Prickly Porky the Porcupine—who carries a thousand little spears. The next book will tell you all about *his* adventures.